ECO-WOLF
and the
THREE PIGS

Written by Laurence Anholt
Illustrated by Arthur Robins

ORCHARD BOOKS
338 Euston Road, London NW1 3BH
Orchard Books Australia
Hachette Children's Books
Level 17/207 Kent St, Sydney, NSW 2000
First published in Great Britain in 1999. This edition published in 2002.
Text © Laurence Anholt 1999. Illustrations © Arthur Robins 1999.
The rights of Laurence Anholt to be identified as the author and
Arthur Robins as the illustrator of this work have been asserted by them
in accordance with the Copyright, Designs and Patents Act, 1988.
A CIP catalogue record for this book is available from the British Library.
ISBN 1 84121 394 2
1 3 5 7 9 10 8 6 4 2
Printed in China

ORCHARD BOOKS

KT-555-920

☆ The Fried Piper ☆ Shampoozel ☆ Daft Jack ☆ The Emperor ☆
☆ Little Red Riding Wolf ☆ Rumply Crumply Stinky Pin ☆

☆ Ghostyshocks ☆ Snow White ☆ Cinderboy ☆ Eco-Wolf ☆
☆ The Greedy Farmer ☆ Billy Beast ☆

In a small wigwam in a beautiful valley lived a gentle creature called Eco-Wolf.

There were no cars or houses in the valley, and Eco-Wolf lived at peace with the trees and the wild animals. He spent his time inventing machines which would make electricity from the clear blue river without causing pollution.

One morning, Eco-Wolf was gently explaining to a young animal about litter.

As they spoke, a huge black car roared into the valley. Out climbed three sinister figures dressed in black. The biggest pig stepped forward:

We're the three pigs and we are BAD,
Greedypig, Grabbit and Megadad.

We don't hang about or dilly-dally,
We're gonna build houses in your valley.

So don't get smart, don't no one get funny,
The pigs are out to make some money.

Eco-Wolf couldn't believe what he was hearing.

"Hey, man," he said, "your car is, like, invading my space. You're messing up the valley vibes, piggy brother."

But the pigs only laughed and set to work.

They built a big ugly straw cottage beside
the river, with a huge satellite dish on the
roof. They had to cut down one or two old
oak trees that were in the way, but the pigs
didn't care about trees.

As they worked the pigs sang very loudly:

Who's afraid of this eco-guy?
If we messed his hair, he'd be sure to cry.

This valley ain't so peaceful no more,
House number one is made of straw.

We're the three pigs, we don't care a fig,
Megadad, Grabbit and Greedypig.

When they had finished, the pigs put
up a 'For Sale' sign and went inside to eat
a HUGE meal.

Eco-Wolf was very sad to see a house beside the blue river, but he was especially sad about the old oak trees. He called the wild animals to his wigwam.

"Hey, wild warrior brother-sisters," said Eco-Wolf. "I don't dig these big pigs. Those trees were kind of like my sister-brothers too. It makes me huff and puff, man."

So Eco-Wolf and his friends walked up to the door of the straw cottage and rang the bell.

"Big Pig, Big Pig," said Eco-Wolf, "like, let me come in."

"Get outa here, buddy," shouted
Megadad, "or you'll get a piggy-punch
on your chinny-chin-chin."

"Then we'll, like, huff and puff, man, and
blow your house sky high," replied Eco-Wolf.

Out of the air came all the wild birds of the valley. They carried away every last piece of straw in their beaks, leaving Greedypig, Grabbit and Megadad with nothing but their TV set.

"That's the last straw. Right, boys?" said
Megadad.

Peace returned to the valley. Eco-Wolf went back to his Eco-Power machine, and the clear river flowed.

But the three bad pigs were making another plan.

"Gather round, boys," said Megadad. "That straw house was a lousy idea. We gotta make somethin' a WHOLE LOT tougher to keep out this Eco-Wolf fella. Right, boys?"

So the bad pigs started work on a wooden
house. It had six bedrooms with double-
glazed windows, a garage, a swimming pool
and a road leading up to it.

The pigs had to dig up some wild flowers and chase a few rabbits out of their homes, but they didn't care about flowers or rabbits.

While they worked, the three pigs sang even louder:

So who's afraid of this eco-freak?
He's a sneaky geek with a whole lotta cheek.

We'll flatten this valley and do it good,
House number two is made of wood.

We're the three pigs, so goodbye rabbit,
Greedypig, Megadad and brother Grabbit.

When they had finished, the three pigs
put up a 'For Sale' sign and went inside to
eat a COLOSSAL meal.

Eco-Wolf was very sad to see another house in the valley, but he was especially sad about the rabbits. He called the wild animals to his wigwam.

"Hey, wild warrior brother-sisters," said Eco-Wolf, "these big pigs are totally uncool. Those rabbits were kind of like my sister-brothers. It makes me huff and puff, man."

So Eco-Wolf and the woodland warriors marched up to the wooden house and rang the bell.

"Big Pig, Big Pig," said Eco-Wolf, "like, let me come in."

"Get outa here, buddy," shouted
Megadad, "or you'll get a chop on your
chinny-chin-chin."

"Then we'll, like, huff and puff, man,
and blow your house into the middle of
next week," replied Eco-Wolf.

Out of the fields came all the underground animals of the valley. They dug tunnels deep under the wooden house until it collapsed, leaving the three pigs in a pile of sawdust.

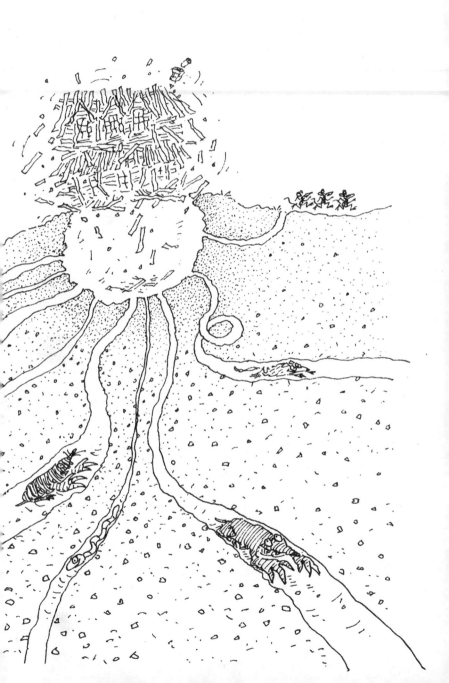

Peace returned once more to the valley.
Eco-Wolf went back to his Eco-Power
machine and the blue river flowed.

But the three bad pigs were making an
even bigger plan.

Eco-Wolf guy. Right, boys?"

So the bad pigs started work again.
This time they used bricks and concrete.
They built a high-rise tower block on top
of a multi-storey shopping centre, with a
motorway leading up to it.

They needed a lot of electricity, so the
three pigs built a huge power station, with
a gigantic chimney, right in the middle of
the valley.

They had to cut down a forest, and the waste from the power station polluted the river, but the pigs didn't care about forests or rivers.

While they worked the three pigs sang
more loudly than ever:

When they had finished, the three pigs put up a 'For Sale' sign and went inside to eat a MEGA meal.

Eco-Wolf looked at the remains of his
beautiful valley. The river was grey, and
the air was black and smoky.

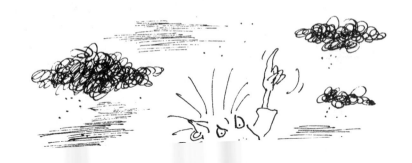

"Hey, wild warrior brother-sisters," he said,
"this valley was, like, my sister-brother, man.
It makes me mad. It makes me ballistic. It
makes me HUFF and PUFF, man."

Eco-Wolf and the wild woodland warriors
stormed up to the power station. There was a
big barbed wire fence all around.

Eco-Wolf pressed the button on the entry-phone.

"Big Pig, Big Pig," he said, "like, let me come in."

"Clear off, or I'll send out the security guards to give you a knuckle sandwich on your chinny-chin-chin," came Megadad's voice.

"Then I'll, like, huff and puff, man, and blow you and your power station into pork scratchings," replied Eco-Wolf.

Deep inside the power station, the three pigs only laughed.

"Hey, wild warriors," said Eco-Wolf, "I'm gonna climb that chimney stack and, like, camp on top, until those big pigs start respecting the planet."

Eco-Wolf strapped his wigwam on to his back. The warrior squirrels scrambled up the fence and pulled Eco-Wolf after them. He began to climb the chimney. It was very high, but Eco-Wolf was brave.

When
he reached
the top, all the
animals cheered.
Eco-Wolf waved once,
unrolled the wigwam,
and sat down to wait.

47

"OK, guys. We'll smoke that wolf out,"
said Megadad. "Right, boys?"

"Right, Dad," replied Greedypig and
Grabbit, pulling a lever which turned the
station to maximum power.

The heat in the power station started to build up. Black smoke poured out of the chimney.

Quick as a flash, Eco-Wolf pulled his wigwam over the top of the chimney so that the smoke drifted back down to the three pigs.

He climbed up inside the chimney, but,
three-quarters of the way up, he got stuck.

"He's too fat," spluttered Grabbit. "I'll go up and get him, Dad."

So Grabbit climbed up inside the chimney, but, halfway up, he got stuck too.

"You're both too fat," shouted Megadad.
"I'll go up and get him."

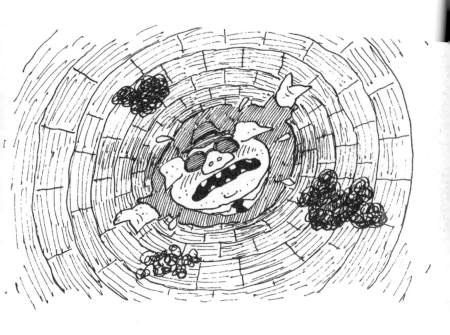

The chimney grew hotter and hotter. The three pigs began to squeal.

Suddenly there was a huge explosion.

Eco-Wolf shot high into the air. Then, holding on to his wigwam like a parachute, he drifted gently to the ground. The three bad pigs were fired out of the chimney like piggy cannon balls.

Greedypig landed in the river.

Grabbit landed on the roof of the big black car.

And Megadad smashed right on to
Eco-Wolf's electricity machine.

The high-rise tower block and every one
of Megadad's buildings exploded into
a thousand tiny pieces.

"Like huff and puff, man. I blew that house down," said Eco-Wolf.

After many days, Eco-Wolf and the
woodland warriors finished clearing up
the valley. The three big pigs were made
to plant new trees and dig new homes for
the rabbits.

5 OOO
NEW
HOMES
FOR
RABBITS

While they worked the three pigs sang
very quietly:

*We're the three pigs and we are sad,
Grabbit, Greedypig and Megadad.*

When they had finished, the three pigs climbed into their car, drove out of the valley and far, far away.

At last, the blue river flowed, and the air was clean again. A young animal asked Eco-Wolf how he would make electricity now that his Eco-Water Power machine was broken.

Eco-Wolf smiled. He was already working on a new idea.